ANGEL'S PRAYER

M. J. PEDERSON

COPYRIGHT INFORMATION:

CHAPTER ONE:

Angel Johnson walked home along the snow-covered sidewalk. Kicking snow with each step, she grew closer and closer to her family's home. While she wandered along, Angel starred down at her boots. They were cool boots. She had wanted them so much, and Daddy had found a way to make sure she got them.

Her feet had not been cold all winter long because they were so warm and comfy. Daddy also made sure Angel's brother, Kyle, got the new coat he needed. Both siblings had noticed their parents' coats were ripped in places, and they were wearing the same old gloves they'd had for years. When she asked her father why they bought new clothes for their children, but not themselves, he explained buying them made them happy. They wanted to give Angel and her brother what they needed.

Angel hoped for a way to buy Mommy and Daddy new gloves and hats for Christmas. Maybe she would ask Kyle if he wanted to do it together. When they put their saved money together, there would surely be enough to get them really warm ones.

Mommy and Daddy did so much for them. When it seemed impossible to make ends meet, they always found a way. Daddy told them it was because they had faith. When they needed something, Mommy read her favorite bible passages and prayed about the item needed or the bill which needed to be paid. She then would leave it up to the Lord and tell him she knew he would help the family. If it was something they needed, the Lord would find a way to help them; and, it seemed He always did.

"That's faith," Daddy had told Angel, "When you believe in your heart and know that the Lord will help, you have faith."

Mommy and Daddy told Angel and her big brother, Kyle, last night that there would not be many presents under the tree this Christmas. It would be a very small and simple Christmas because their father had lost his job earlier that year.

The family barley had enough to get by and had to use food stamps, donations from churches and money from odd jobs to pay bills and buy food; However, once again her parents were strong in faith and this was an example to Angel. She prayed every night for some kind of Christmas with her annual sleep over and a few gifts. The traditions were most important to Angel. It was the special, little things which made it feel like Christmas.

Angel walked along the curb to the Johnson's street. It was a nice street. Lots of kids to play with and Christmas decorations were up and down the street. Everyone decorated their homes on Ankeny Street. She looked down the sidewalk to her family's house. It was beautiful.

The upstairs held Kyle and Angel's rooms. In the main floor were a bathroom, living room, family room and big kitchen. The basement was nice too; not like one of those old scary basements her friends had or she saw on movies. It was really nice with brown carpet and a couch, chair, old television, and stereo. Mommy's washer and dryer were on one side of the basement. And, in the corner, was Daddy's old desk which now held Angel's journal and notebooks of stories and poems.

Sometimes Angel would go down, turn on some country music and write stories or poetry... it all depended on her mood. No matter how bad school was, or how many worries she had, things seemed better in her little corner of the basement. Angel would lose herself in her characters. Writing was her way to forget for a while. But, as soon as she put away her pen, closed her notebook, and hid it in the bottom drawer of the desk, Angel would have to walk up the stairs to the kitchen and back to reality.

The snow started falling harder with the big huge flakes bringing Angel back from daydreaming. She walked along, her backpack hanging on her elbows. Her head was facing the sky with her eyes closed. She let snowflakes fall on her tongue. Angel loved catching snowflakes; it was one of her favorite things about winter. If they didn't have a great Christmas, at least they would have snow!

When Angel reached the yard, she threw her backpack down on the sidewalk. She turned and plopped down in the snow. Falling back, Angel spreading her arms wide, like an angel. Moving them up and down as her legs shuffled in and out very fast, she created wings. Angel loved making snow angels, especially at Christmas. The snow seemed so full of magic at Christmas. And, after all, her name was Angel!

After finishing her masterpiece Angel got up very slowly. But when she looked down, she saw her hand and knee print. When she had stood, her knee had made a mark on the leg and her hand print was right in the middle of the angel she had worked so hard on. Her smile was replaced with a frown. Suddenly, a shadow of a man moved over the angel. The shadow waved at her and, smiling again, Angel turned around. Daddy was standing behind her. He was a tall man with blonde hair and blue eyes just like Angel and Kyle.

"What's the matter darling? Did your snow angel get messed up again?" he asked, smiling down at her.

Daddy picked up some handfuls of snow and placed them into the flaws on the snow angel. He moved his hands around and blended the frozen water in. Then, when he stood up a beautiful snow angel was in front of them.

"You're my Angel," Daddy said winking.

He took Angel's hand; handed the backpack to her and they walked into the house through the big front door. The sweet smell of hot chocolate greeting them as they entered.

"Honey, we're home!" Daddy and Angel cried in unison. Daddy set Angel down and hung up his coat.

She took off her snow pants, boots, gloves, hat, scarf and coat. She was warm, but her nose and cheeks were still red from being out in the cold. Mommy came into the living room carrying three mugs of her famous hot chocolate with a special Christmas treat of marshmallows. Daddy had started a fire in the wood burning stove which sat in the corner of their living room.

Daddy looked at Mommy and she stared back as if she were asking a question. Then Angel saw her father shake his head and her mother frown a little. Going over to Mommy he put his arms around her, stared into her eyes, and somehow this made Mommy feel better without saying a word. He gave her a big hug.

"Next time babe. The Lord will send me a job, have faith."

Angel guessed this meant Daddy's interview didn't go well. He needed and wanted a job so bad. Daddy got up and hung Angel's gloves, hat and scarf, near the fire to dry.

"How was school honey?" Mommy asked as she took a big gulp of hot chocolate.

Both Daddy and Angel laughed because when the older woman looked at them, she had marshmallow goo all over her upper lip. Realizing what they were laughing at, Mommy made a funny face, crossing her eyes and sticking her tongue out. Then, she wiped off the marshmallow goo with a napkin.

While they were all laughing the front door swung open. Kyle walked in carrying his football. Kyle always had a football in his hands. He loved the game and dreamed of being a professional player someday. He played for his school team and his coach said her brother had a lot of talent for someone his age.

Being only thirteen years old, Kyle didn't care about much, except for football. Though Angel had noticed lately, her brother made sure he looked good before school and was even wearing cologne. Angel was twelve years old and had crushes in school, but still really only cared about her writing.

"Well guys its Friday. The weekend is finally here. And, to-morrow we are all going to Grandpa's farm to help him cut down his Christmas tree. We're gonna cut one down for ourselves too. After we're done helping Grandpa decorate his tree, we'll come home to decorate ours," Mommy told them.

Angel loved going to Grandpa Montgomery's to get their tree. They went into the woods and cut them down themselves. They didn't go to a Christmas tree lot or set up a fake one. Only real and only the best!

The rest of the night was spent watching movies and eating popcorn. Angel always loved Friday nights; everyone was so happy and relaxed. After a couple Christmas movies Mommy told everyone to head to bed. It was going to be a busy day to-morrow.

Angel went into her bedroom and put on her flannel night-gown. She kneeled beside her bed to say goodnight to Jesus and prayed for her parents, brother, Grandpa and that Christmas would bring them all they needed. Then she told Him what she wished for, her dreams.

"Amen," Angel finished and climbed into her bed. Pulling her pink quilt up to her chin she closed her eyes and drifted off to sleep. That night Angel's dreams were filled with pine trees, horses and snow.

CHAPTER TWO:

The next morning Angel woke early. For some reason, she felt drawn to look out the window first thing. She gasped at what she saw. It had snowed overnight. There was snow everywhere. The trees were covered, and it looked really deep. This was the best kind of snow, deep and hopefully good packing. Maybe there would be enough to make a snowman.

She dressed in a hurry, including thermal underwear under her clothes. She learned last year that hunting trees with Grandpa can not only take a long time, but be *very* cold! So, this year she decided she would be prepared. After she finished dressing, Angel hurried down the open stairway to the kitchen for breakfast.

Each year Mommy made a special breakfast on tree hunting day. Pancakes, sausage, bacon, eggs, hash browns, orange juice, and of course, hot chocolate was on the table waiting when she took her seat.

"You look ready to go, Angel," Mommy said to her. She also said today was supposed to be cold, so it was good thinking that Angel had bundled up.

"Yep, I remember last year, Mommy. I'm not gonna get cold this year. So, when do we leave?" Angel asked.

"We head out as soon as your brother and Daddy are ready. Daddy is in the shower and Kyle is just getting out of bed," Mommy said dishing up some eggs and hash browns for herself.

Angel was handed a plate of hot buttered biscuits smothered in sausage gravy. Yummy, her favorite. While Angel was sipping her hot chocolate Daddy and Kyle came down to the kitchen. They dished up their plates and ate quickly, because they all knew Grandpa liked to get started early, and they still had an hour drive ahead of them.

After everyone finished their meal the family loaded into their SUV and set out for Grandpa's farm. Angel was bursting with excitement. She couldn't wait to get on the horses and set out to find the perfect trees. This was one of her favorite parts of Christmas. The drive to Grandpa's was about an hour so Angel was hardly able to control herself by the time they pulled into his long, winding lane. Then, the farmhouse came into view with smoke billowing from the chimney. Christmas was officially here!

Angel jumped out of the car first and was greeted by Rex, Grandpa's dog. She patted his head and then ran up to the porch to knock and let Grandpa know they had arrived. The door opened and there stood all six feet of him in his old overalls and brown leather cap. He was ready to go.

"C'mon, Pumpkin! Let's go get those horses ready," Grandpa said to Angel, taking her by the hand and leading her to the stable.

Angel loved her Grandpa's horses, especially the one she named Midnight. It was beautiful; the darkest black anyone could imagine. He reminded her of the late-night sky. Midnight had a few white specks on him which looked like the stars in the sky, especially on the nights she and Grandma use to go out.

Sometimes when it was snowing, Angel woke up early in the morning before the sun came up. Those nights she and Grandma would sneak out while the family slept. They would stand very quietly in their boots and coats with their night-gowns on underneath. You could actually hear the snow fall. It was so peaceful and pretty. This was how Angel would always re-member Grandma. Grandma had died two year ago and everyone missed her. That is why Angel named the horse Midnight and was the one who rode her.

Angel and Grandpa got the horses ready and the rest of the family joined them. They all saddled up and set out to ride into Grandpa's wooded land. The hunt for two perfect trees was on! This was the fun part. They rode and rode, talking and enjoying the snow. As they trotted around the wooded area on Grandpa's land, they sang Christmas Carols and laughed. All of their cheeks and noses were red and it was freezing cold. None of them seemed to care though, because they were having such a good time.

This was the fun part of Christmas. This is what Angel looked forward to the most. It signaled the season for their family, kicked all the celebrations off. After finding the perfect trees, they would drag them back behind their horses, then would have hot chocolate and homemade cookies while they helped Grandpa decorate his tree.

The hunt took a while. Like Grandpa said, "Can't just cut down the first one ya see. Have to hunt, search, and look close till that perfect tree is there before you."

Everyone continued singing carols and having a good time with Angel and Grandpa leading the way. After her off key and loud rendition of Silent Night, Angel asked Grandpa how they would know which tree was the right one. They had so many to choose from.

"We'll know Angel. It will speak to us. We'll all just know that this is the tree destined to help us celebrate this Christmas, celebrate Jesus's birth," Grandpa said with a smile.

So the family continued their hunt. Finally, they found their tree; it was standing before them in the middle of Grandpa's land. He had been right; it spoke to Angel. This was the tree! Even more special was the fact that there were two of them, standing next to each other. Side by side, just like Grandpa and Angel were; they were not only grandfather and granddaughter, they were best friends!

The trees were not too small and not too big. Full and

perfect, they stood there before them. Grandpa, Daddy, and Kyle chopped down the trees and tied them behind Grandpa and Daddy's horses. Dragging the trees behind them, the family made their way back to the house, with their voices trailing behind them as they sang "Jingle Bells".

Mommy and Angel went into the kitchen to make hot chocolate with marshmallows, coffee, and set out the tray of cookies. They also popped popcorn to string and found some cranberries to use. Grandpa liked the old-fashioned homemade ornaments. A simple life had always been the best for Grandpa. It was the only way he wanted to live. No computers, no cable, no compact disc players or DVDs. Just a radio, small television and phone in his log cabin; this was all Grandpa would ever need. And, of course, the love of his family.

Grandpa, Daddy and Kyle set Grandpa's tree up in the living room and Daddy made a nice fire in the fireplace. When Angel and Mommy entered the room, the fire was burning and it was getting nice and toasty warm in the small room. Everyone still had red cheeks and noses though, but the cold fresh air had felt great. Angel would not have changed the day at all. She had loved every minute of it.

The tree was up in its stand and some simple white lights were already strung. Angel opened the box of ornaments from when her Mommy was a little girl, as well as the ones from Kyle and her childhoods so far. One by one each ornament was hung on a branch. The room smelled of pine, cookies, and hot chocolate. And, little by little, with each glittered ornament which had been made with love, the tree was decorated. Each year of their lives was represented and relived as they hung each one carefully.

"This is what Christmas is supposed to smell like," thought Angel to herself as she hung an ornament she'd made of yarn and popsicle sticks three years earlier.

This was what she wanted when she grew up. A simple life on a farm. It was the perfect life to live. Everything calm and relaxed. No problems or worries to complicate life. Money and jobs did not enter the picture when they were at Grandpa's. He always told Daddy to keep the faith, because things have a way of working out. The Lord has a plan for each of us and will make sure we follow His plan.

Each ornament was finally hanging on the tree along with some candy canes. Strings of popcorn, cranberries and chains made from construction paper clung lightly to the green branches. It looked perfect. As the sun set, all that lit the living room was the light from the fireplace and brightness of the white Christmas lights on the tree. It was so pretty and Angel felt really happy. The happiest she had felt in a very long time.

Eventually it was time to leave Grandpa's and go home. Back to the problems of life. She always felt so safe and secure at the farm. They tied their tree to the top of their SUV and loaded it for the trip home, then it would be time for more hot chocolate and to decorate their own Christmas tree.

The ride home was fun. Everyone sang Christmas carols again and talked about their favorite memories. Mommy and Daddy reminded them, this year was going to be a simple Christmas, but that didn't mean it wasn't going to be special. It could even end up being the best Christmas ever. They were not going to focus on gifts this year, but on the real meaning of Christmas; the birth of Jesus.

"I know what I want for Christmas Mommy and Daddy!" Angel said from the backseat.

She had been half listening and looking out the window. She watched as the empty fields passed by, dried stalks of corn poking through the blanket of snow which had fallen. The darkness was apparent as the sun set more and more. Christmas lights were being turned on at the houses they drove past.

"What's your Christmas wish honey?" Mommy asked.

"It's not really a wish Mommy," Angel said.

"Well, what is it you want then honey?" her Daddy asked.

"I want Daddy to find the job he wants. A job he likes and

all the worries to go away," Angel said. Actually, it just came out. She wasn't thinking. It just went right from her thoughts, out her mouth, and into the conversation.

"That would be great Angel, but you must want something for yourself," Daddy said.

"No, Daddy. I want you to get a job, and all of us to be happy again; not having to worry all the time," Angel stated.

She was serious. She wanted nothing more than this simple wish. This was her heart's desire. The one thing she wished for most in the world. Driving down that small rural highway to her house, she said a prayer hoping it would come true. This was not something Santa could handle. She turned to the one who always helped and was always there. He is the one true best friend who would be there through every day of her life, the Lord.

"Thank you, honey. That means more to us than you know," Daddy said with a big smile. When Angel looked over at Mommy, she saw her wipe a tear from her eye.

The SUV then turned onto the street where they lived. All the houses were lit, Christmas was definitely on its way. Angel felt a warmth inside that she had never felt before. It was like the way she felt when she was at Grandpa's farm. It was a safe feeling and of being loved.

The family pulled into the drive on Ankeny Street. Angel put on her gloves; it was really cold out. While she walked to the front door with Mommy, she could see her breath. She knew everything would all work out and be fine. The Lord would work his wonders.

"Maybe this is what faith is," Angel thought to herself. Can you really feel faith? Something inside her said yes.

Opening the door Mommy and Angel turned on the lights before going to the basement to dig out the boxes of ornaments and Christmas decorations. Daddy and Kyle brought in the tree and set it up in the corner of the living room. While they were getting boxes down from the shelf Daddy had built in the basement, Angel heard Daddy's Elvis Christmas record on the old record player. Angel carried up boxes of ornaments while humming along to Blue Christmas.

Christmas tradition was always followed in the Johnson home. The first decoration put up was Mommy's beautiful manger and nativity scene. There was a statue of Mary, one of Joseph, and of course one of baby Jesus. The manger was made of special wood that gave it a very old look. Mommy and Angel sprinkled pretend snow on the top of the manger. The last part of the manger to be set out was a beautiful angel which was bought the year Angel had been born. This was the first decoration every year because it represented why they were celebrating Christmas... The birth of our King.

For the next few hours, the family decorated the tree. Memories flooded forward as each ornament was hung on a prickly pine branch. Angel remembered opening her Santa on the sled ornament a few years back. She had chicken pox at Christmas, so it wasn't very fun. She couldn't cut down the trees or other favorite traditions. She didn't even get to go sit on Santa's lap. She went to bed one night, crying. When she woke the next morning there was a candy cane on her bedside table. And, next to the candy cane was the cutest little Santa on a sled.

Angel hung the ornament on a bottom branch and looked at Kyle who was holding a football ornament from the same year. They both smiled at each other and giggled. This was what Christmas was; family, fun and memories to fill each day.

The rest of the weekend went by fast. Mommy and Angel made bunches of candies, cookies and of course, fudge. They had also made the rolls for Christmas dinner as well as pumpkin and apple pies. They would freeze the pies until Christmas morning. Early in the morning Mommy would get up and take the pies out to thaw. Time was always something that went fast this time of year. Between cooking, shopping, decorating and going to Christmas plays and programs, their schedules were very busy.

No matter how busy each of them were they would gather

around the dinner table every night for supper. Bowing their heads, they thanked the Lord for the food before them and for the roof over their heads. Special prayers were said for Daddy's job search and a few other people from the parish that were ill.

Sunday night it started snowing again. Angel went to bed hoping that when she looked out the window the next morning there would be tons of snow. She so wanted a snow day. A day of sledding and play outside all day long is just what she needed.

Monday morning greeted Angel with just a dusting of snow and an on-time school start.

"Rise and shine," Mommy yelled up at Angel from the bottom of the stairs.

"I'm up mom, just getting dressed," Angel yelled back.

"Ok, but hurry up, you're running late. You need to eat and the bus is due here soon," Mommy called back up.

Angel finished getting ready while humming "Jingle Bells".

CHAPTER THREE:

Angel looked over at her alarm clock. She was late. All this daydreaming made her have to hurry. Sometimes she'd just sit in bed and think of ideas for stories. She actually kept a notebook by her bed and wrote down her ideas and thoughts when they came. Mommy loved reading all of her stories and Daddy said that she would be the next JK Rowling. Their words meant so much to Angel since JK Rowling was her idol.

Angel opened her closet door and picked out a nice red skirt and sweater set. She wore a white turtleneck under the sweater. After a few minutes of fumbling in her jewelry box Angel found the Christmas tree pin that Grandma had given her. She pinned it on her sweater and pulled her hair back into a ponytail.

Today all the classes were practicing and choosing parts for the school Christmas program. Most girls desperately wanted to be Mary in the program, but Angel wanted nothing more than wear the white sheet with tinsel around the bottom that signified an angel. She desperately hoped for a halo made of gold garland secured above her head.

Since she was a baby, Angel had loved angels and always would. Quickly she said a prayer asking the Lord to let her be the angel. It was perfect for her; she was named Angel, so it was fate! If only Sister Mary Violet could see that!

Angel and Kyle both went to a small Christian school called St. John. When they first began school, it was great. But, many of the students have parents that make lots of money. Now with Daddy not working and Angel and Kyle having to wear hand me downs, they both went through a lot. The kids teased Angel in her class all that year, but it was Christmas now, so who cared!

"Come on guys, cream of wheat this morning!" Mommy called up.

Angel heard Kyle's door open and him running down the stairs. He loved Cream of Wheat. She thought it was ok, but she would rather have hash browns and bacon. Each week on Monday Mommy made a special breakfast. Last week had been Angel's breakfast and this week was Kyle's. Daddy always had pancakes and sausage. And, when it was Mommy's turn, she said all she wanted was a package of donuts, so she didn't have to cook. So, they usually had a variety of donuts Daddy bought at the local bakery before they all woke up. This way Mommy didn't have to go out in the cold, and she didn't have to do dishes on her breakfast day.

Kyle had already finished his first bowl and was getting ready to go dish up seconds when Angel walked into the kitchen. He put tons of butter, cinnamon and sugar on his Cream of Wheat and mixed it all up really good. Daddy sat across from Kyle, slowly pouring milk over his clump of Cream of Wheat, then sprinkled sugar over it. Angel preferred Kyle's way of fixing the dish, so she sat down and began by sprinkling cinnamon on the cereal.

"Anything interesting going on at school today kids?" Mommy asked as she sipped her cappuccino. Monday was also Mommy's cappuccino day. She thought it was a good way to start the week. Often, she would reflect and read her scriptures after everyone left the house on Mondays. It was her special time with the Lord.

"Yeah, they're picking the parts for the school Christmas program," Kyle said.

He didn't really care what part he was given, as long as he didn't have to sing a solo. Kyle was actually a wonderful singer, was offered solo after solo, but he would never take the part. He hated crowds and had terrible stage fright. So, instead you could always spot him in the back row belting out a beautiful rendition of the song which was being sung. His voice could always be heard over the rest of the choir. He was fine, so long as he had the protection of the whole choir around him.

"That's right, let's see you're in sixth grade now, Angel; isn't that the grade that does the nativity scene?" Daddy asked.

He knew it was the grade. Every girl at St. John couldn't wait to be in sixth grade.

Mommy cleared the dishes off the table and started loading them in the dishwasher as Angel and Kyle put their books in their bags. Then, slipping on their coats, boots and other winter wear, they both headed to the bus stop. It was still snowing lightly, but very small light flakes; more like flurries. Angel still wished they would have a big snowstorm.

She loved snowstorms. If it was bad enough the most of the town would shut down. Snowmobiles and four wheelers drove through the streets of town; people had to walk to go places like the store, because there was so much snow everywhere. And, there were always hours of playing in the snow; building snow people, sledding, snow ball fights and building snow forts. After a long day of playing hard in the snow Kyle and Angel would find big cups of hot chocolate with marshmallows when they returned inside. It was great and Angel was in the mood for some fun in the snow!

The school bus rounded the corner and headed for them. One by one the kids from her neighborhood got on the bus including Angel's best friends Christie, Pam, and Jolene. The girls took up two seats near the back and started talking about their Christmas wishes. Angel listened as they talked of CD players, televisions and computers. How could she tell them her one and only wish was for Daddy to find a great job so he would be really happy and funny again. So, they would have enough money to buy everything they needed. There was no way they could ever understand.

All three of her friends were from families with money. Not rich, but they never had to worry about the things Angel's family did, and they got special surprises all the time. They actually expected them. So, when they turned to Angel, she said she wanted a CD player and a professional pen set. They said that was cool and to Angel's relief changed the topic to boys. They all compared the boys on the bus each day. Well, the ones their age and those a couple years older.

Kyle, with his football in hand, sat with his friends from the team. Angel always thought Perry was the cutest of the boys from the team; but Kyle didn't hang with him that much. His best friends were from his home room; Randy, Kevin, Denny, and Keith. They all loved football, cars, and girls.

"I'm so excited about the Christmas program," Christie said.

Christie was a nice girl who would turn twelve in a couple months. She had black naturally wavy hair, which she instead wore as a short mess of curls. Her eyes were blue like Angels but a weird shade, almost crystal blue. They were so pretty. She was tall also and had great clothes. The one thing Christie and Angel had in common that none of the other girls did, was their love for writing and reading as well as for ponies and horses. Christie's parents were going to be getting her a horse in a few months, and she promised Angel that she could come over and ride it as often as she liked.

Pam was a very outspoken girl. She had long blonde hair which she wore down and sometimes had two small braids in front. Her hair was always so shiny. She had green eyes and was just a little shorter than Angel. She always wore jeans and cowgirl boots. Even when it was as cold as this, she brought them to school with her to change into. Pam was also a great singer and would probably be singing the solo at the school program for their grade.

Jolene was a very nice girl. She had red hair that was kind

of frizzy and down to her shoulders. She had green eyes too, but wore glasses so it was hard to see them. Jolene was a little plump, but Mommy said it wasn't overweight. It was more like filling out. Compared to the other girls in the class, Jolene seemed to be sprinting to adolescence while the others were just taking their time. Jolene couldn't wait to have her first date and kiss. And, she was the most excited about the upcoming dance.

"What do you think Angel? What do you want to be picked to do for the program?" Pam asked bringing Angel back to reality.

"There she goes day dreaming again, and it's still before nine. Were you thinking up a story?" Jolene asked as she looked into the mirror she was holding, trying carefully to apply a thin layer of lipstick while the bus bounced down the street.

"Jolene, you should wait and do that at school or while we're stopped. You're going to get it all over yourself!" Christie said.

"I'm ok; I've been doing this for a while. Don't worry, I know how to do it right without messing it up," Jolene said. But, in reality, Jolene had only been wearing lipstick for three weeks now and had to keep it hidden from her parents. They didn't want her wearing any make up until eighth grade, but Jolene went to the dollar store and purchased a hot pink color.

"I don't know. Truthfully the part I most hoped for is the angel," Angel said smiling.

They all knew it. That was all she talked about each Christmas play since she saw her first one. All the girls were oohing over Mary; but, not Angel. She loved the costume and the importance of the angel. Not only because of her name, but she loved them, and had always been fascinated by them. She knew that there were angels around and knew her guardian angel always watched over her.

"Well, I'm going to get Mary. I have the right look and stage presence for her," Jolene said. She was in the school play last year. She walked on the stage and said "the phone sir" and then walked

Angel's lips and said blot.

"What?" Angel asked.

"Like this," Jolene said showing her how to press her lips on the towel lightly to get the excess lipstick off and make it look more natural.

"Wow," was all Angel could say. She didn't realize that such a little amount of make-up could make her look so very different.

"You look great!" Jolene said.

Truthfully knowing she looked pretty, gave Angel a better attitude. She walked to the classroom with more confidence and a big smile. Maybe she would get the part of the angel, Daddy would get his job, and maybe, just maybe, Santa would bring her some lipstick for Christmas.

As she walked into homeroom, she noticed Pam and Christie's mouths drop open. Jolene had been the first and only girl to wear make-up in school yet. No one thought Angel would try it. They thought she'd be the last. She wasn't into that type of stuff. Her blonde hair had always been pulled back into a ponytail and braided. She usually wore jeans and t-shirts in school or turtle necks with flannels over them. But first a skirt and sweater set and now make-up. Her friends couldn't believe their eyes. She had also let her hair down and brushed it out.

As Angel made her way to her seat she sat down. Pulling out her books she looked at Christie who whispered, "What happened?"

Angel shrugged her shoulders, smiled at her and then went back to preparing for class.

Angel loved the first class of the day. It was Creative Writing and she was getting an A. This was without even trying. She loved to write and her teacher, Ms. Doyle, loved reading her work. It was also a class that required journal writing. The other kids only wrote the minimum they had to. Not Angel, she had already filled a couple books.

She journaled during the class and also study hall and any other breaks during the day. It was her "school journal" which she only wrote in at school. Then she had her "special journal" in the basement at home that held her most personal thoughts and feelings. She loved journaling. It helped a lot, especially when she was sad or mad.

Angel had been writing for a good five minutes when Ms. Doyle came in and said good morning. She set down her pen and put on her glasses. Then, like she did a lot throughout the day, she turned and snuck a look at Mark Adams. He was the cutest and one of the biggest crushes she had ever had. Usually when she looked, he was looking somewhere else or talking to his friends. But this time, he was staring right at her. When he realized she had caught him, he looked away really fast.

"First make-up, and now Mark is looking at me? This may be a great day!" Angel thought to herself.

"Ok, class, attention! Class! Ok, everyone, stop talking!" Ms. Doyle said over the roar of the students. After a few attempts it worked and the classroom was once again silent.

"I hope you all have finished your journaling because first thing this morning we are going to draw for parts in the school program. Everyone, write your name on a piece of paper and I'm going to pass around two baskets, one for girls and one for boys. Put your names in the correct basket and pass them to the next person. Please make it fast boys and girls because we need to go to practice soon," Ms. Doyle said with a smile as she handed Jackie Duwa the basket.

The process of putting their names in went very fast, and as the basket was picked up by Ms. Doyle, you could see how nervous the girls were. The boys looked like they didn't care; but, when Ms. Doyle announced that the first part, she would be drawing for would be Joseph, Angel noticed a lot of the boys were sitting up straight and listening very close.

"Ok, this year Joseph will be..."" Ms. Doyle said as she fished around in the boys' basket.

"MARK ADAMS!" she said loudly with a smile.

The class clapped and Mark got up and walked to the front to get his costume from Ms. Doyle's teacher assistant, Michelle.

"The three wise men will be…" Angel heard Ms. Doyle say before she got lost in another daydream.

Angel thought it would be great to be Mary too, especially if Mark was Joseph. She could get to talk to him and get to know him better. Mark had just moved to Iowa a couple months ago. He didn't talk a lot, so not many people knew much about him.

"And this year's Mary will be…" Ms. Doyle said.

"JACKIE DUWA!" she said loudly again with a smile.

Jackie yelled yeah and her friends were all clapping for her. Angel didn't like Jackie very much. She was one of the kids that made fun of her, because her Daddy didn't have a job, and she had to wear hand me down clothes. Sometimes she told everyone that the outfit or shirt that Angel was wearing was bought at the Goodwill. She said she knew it because her Mom had given it to them last week.

When she said this, the kids laughed, and it made Angel want to cry. She had always been nice to Jackie and didn't understand why she wanted to hurt her so much. And, when she told the teacher or her parents or tried to stick up for herself, the teasing got worse. So, she just stayed away from Jackie and her click of friends.

"Jackie; she did NOT deserve to be Mary" Angel thought to herself.

"Our head angel this year is…" Ms. Doyle continued on.

"ANGEL JOHNSON!" she said.

Angel felt herself smile as Pam, Christie and Jolene all clapped for her. And, as she looked up front, she saw Mark was even smiling and clapping as loud as her friends.

Pam, Christie and Jolene were also angels, but in the Angel

Choir. Angel was the head angel, meaning she would be standing behind Mark and Jackie. The cool thing too about the nativity scene is they used a real baby.

During practice Jackie was sitting on the stool holding the baby and Mark was standing next to her. Angel had done a lot of babysitting at her house for her Uncle Mike's baby with Mommy's help. This was how she saved up her money for Christmas gifts this year.

The baby started crying while Jackie was holding him, so Angel leaned over behind Jackie and started cooing and talking to the baby. It worked and the baby drifted off the sleep. They practiced all the lines and their songs. Afterwards, they were all released for lunch.

Angel and the girls started heading to the cafeteria. They had smelled the aroma of pizza all morning long. The school made the best cheese pizza; Angel would choose it over one from a restaurant any day!

"Angel, you were really great back there," someone said behind her.

They had just gotten in the lunch line. When she and the girls turned around, they saw Mark standing there. His hands were tucked in his pockets, and he was shifting his weight from one foot to the other. If she didn't know any better, Angel would swear he was nervous.

The girls nudged Angel closer to Mark and stepped a little farther up in the line. They were far enough away to not be in the way of their conversation, but close enough to listen in.

"Thanks, but what do you mean? All I had to do was stand there behind you and Jackie and pretend to sing," Angel said.

Mark laughed and shook his head. He had noticed before that Angel could be funny.

"No, I mean with the baby. Jackie looked like she was about to lose it. It had only just started fussing, and I thought she was going to get up and walk off the altar," he said.

"Oh that, I forgot. Yeah, he was the cutest little baby. He was just scared, all the new people. That or he wanted attention, and just needed someone to talk to," Angel said smiling.

Mark smiled back as Angel looked down at her feet, playing with a pen cap which had fallen on the floor.

They both kept talking as they moved forward with the line. Next thing she knew they were giving Mrs. Bundy their lunch tickets while they got their milk and silverware. Mark handed her a carton of milk and Angel handed him some silverware and a straw.

"I've been babysitting for my uncle's baby. I guess it makes me more relaxed around them. I think he was just tired and fussy. If Jackie would have just talked to him a bit and rocked him back and forth, he would have drifted off to sleep for her," Angel said, as she chose two slices of pizza, corn, fruit cocktail and a chocolate brownie.

"Yeah, but I don't think Jackie's the type to do that. She only cares about how things are going for her, not other people," Mark said.

"I don't understand people like that. They can make another person's life so miserable. That is not what the Lord wanted. He wanted us all to get along and care about each other. I don't think he had in mind what goes on now when he created the world. I just wish people like Jackie would get a taste of their own medicine someday. You know, like the saying goes, 'Do unto others as you would have others do unto you'," Angel said.

She had been so comfortable talking with Mark, she suddenly realized she was almost preaching again. She had the tendency to do this. But apparently Mark did not mind.

"I know, she will someday," he said smiling.

They had finished getting their trays and were standing at the condiments table.

"Well, I should go sit with the girls," Angel said.

"Yeah, the guys are waiting for me," Mark said.

"Well, till science then. Remember we have a quiz!" Angel said smiling.

She then turned and walked to the table where Jolene was talking to Pam about math homework. Christie looked totally bored. That is, until Angel sat down.

"Ok, what was that all about?" Christie asked immediately.

Pam and Jolene both nodded their heads and leaned in closer.

"He just said I did a good job calming the baby in practice. Nothing else. Oh, and something about the science quiz," Angel said. Ok, it was a little white lie, but at least now they wouldn't bug her about him coming up to talk to her.

Angel looked over at Mark who was again staring her way. But this time he didn't turn away. Instead he smiled and waved. She waved back without the girls seeing and picked up her pizza taking a big bite.

This was shaping up to be a great Monday. One of the best she'd had in a long time.

CHAPTER FOUR:

"Mommy I'm home," Angel yelled walking through the front door and setting her book bag down.

Immediately she could tell that her Mom had been busy all day with Christmas preparations. There were more decorations up along the banister and windows. She had also been making candy. The aroma of chocolate filled the house.

"I'm in here, Angel," Mommy yelled from the kitchen.

Angel walked into the kitchen to see her mother covered in flour fighting with the chocolate in the double broiler. Every year she made tons and tons of candies. And, she always used the same double broiler, the one that had been Grandma's.

This year the family had been unsure if they'd even be able to make the traditional Christmas treats. They barely had enough food to make dinner each night. Grandpa had sent a check for the ingredients, because he liked Mommies goodies so much.

"It isn't Christmas without your delicious treats. They are one of my favorite Christmas traditions. Times may be tough but remember to trust in the Lord. 'God will take care of your tomorrow too. Live one day at a time.' Matthew 6:34," he had written in the card.

"Smells yummy, Mommy," Angel said as she took a seat on a stool by the island in the kitchen.

"Hope it tastes that way too!" Mommy said giggling.

But, Mommy's candies, cookies and goodies always tasted perfect. When Angel took them to school for the Class Christmas Party each year, they were the first to be devoured. They always knew which ones were the treats Angel's Mommy had made.

In fact, Angel's best friend's families each got a red or green plastic plate loaded with goodies from the Johnson kitchen. It was always wrapped in red plastic wrap and had ribbon typing it shut. Mommy made sure the baskets and gifts she gave away looked really festive. It was so much fun for her, she loved it!

"So, don't leave me in suspense, Angel. What part did you get?" Mommy asked, secretly hoping it would be the part of Mary.

"I'm the Head Angel, Mommy. I think it's perfect for me, and not just because of my name. I love angels Mommy and always have wanted to be the Head Angel since I saw the first program in kindergarten. I'm in the nativity scene of course, right by Mary and Joseph," Angel said, conveniently forgetting to tell Mommy about who was playing Joseph and what had happened that day at lunch.

Mommy was pretty ok when it came to friends, but when it came to boys, she was really protective, sometimes overprotective. At least she had Daddy in her corner when it came to the overprotective stuff. She did sense there would be a fight about her going to the dance with a boy and not her friends. Angel didn't want to deal with it right then and continued talking about her day.

"That's wonderful honey. I know it was the part you wanted. Did any of the girls your friends with get the part," Mommy asked dipping pretzels into the melted chocolate.

"No, they are also angels, but in the choir. I'm the only angel that will be directly in the nativity scene. Oh, and the play is going to be at 7pm on December 18th Mommy. I can't wait, but it is real soon isn't it," Angel said smiling while she sneaked a peanut cluster from the container Mommy had stored them in.

"Yes, it is not that long away is it? I guess we'd better get going on a dress for you. What do you want to wear this year?" Mommy asked. Each year she and Mommy either found a dress at their favorite store or made one if they had enough time.

Angel really wanted a new dress. But they really couldn't afford it. Besides, she would be wearing the angel costume, which would cover what she was wearing. So, it was not really import-ant. And, she was head angel; a new outfit didn't mean a lot. She had gotten what she wanted!

"Don't worry about my outfit Mommy. The angel costume will cover up what I'm wearing anyway. I'll just wear something I already have," Angel said, this time sneaking a Christmas cookie.

"Oh no you won't. We always buy a new outfit or make something. So, what are you thinking about this year, what are you leaning towards? Are we going with a skirt and blouse or a dress?" Mommy asked as she went to the freezer to put the next batch of chocolate covered pretzels into set.

"I don't know Mommy. What do you think?" Angel asked.

"I think a dress. You look great in them, and we could go find one at the mall tonight after dinner," Mommy said.

What Angel didn't know is that Mommy had prayed for the last two weeks for a way to get her the outfit for her Christ-mas play like they always had. Daddy and Mommy had prayed each night after reading the scriptures before bed. They still had faith, but were getting worried knowing that they had to buy her the outfit soon. Then, when they checked the mail that morning there had been a card from Grandpa telling them to get each of the kids' new outfits for the Christmas play, because he wanted to watch them perform this year.

"Oh, Mommy! Thank you!" Angel said.

"I better go get my homework done before dinner so we can leave right after the dishes are done," Angel said grabbing her book bag and heading up the stairs to her room.

Thankfully there wasn't a lot to do for homework that night. Angel had finished her math and social studies assign-ments. She was working on an essay for creative writing when there was a knock on the door.

"Come in," Angel said.

"Hey, Mom sent me up to tell you dinner is almost ready," Kyle said taking a seat on Angel's beanbag chair by her over stuffed bookshelf.

Kyle watched Angel while she worked on her essay.

"You really like writing don't you. I knew you were good at it, but you're actually smiling," he said.

"Yep, it's fun and it helps me escape from all the stuff that goes on," Angel said trying to explain what she hadn't yet figured out how to explain to anyone.

"I know what you mean. Football is that way for me. When I'm at practice or playing in a game nothing bothers me. I'm just… happy," Kyle said with a smile.

Kyle and Angel were like most brothers and sisters. They had their arguments, sometimes bugged each other a lot, but deep down loved and worried about each other.

"So, where have you been?" Angel asked as she finished the essay and began putting away her school things.

"Dad took me to get a new shirt and pants for the Christmas play," Kyle said smiling.

What Kyle didn't tell Angel is that he and Dad had picked out the clothes pretty fast. He'd picked out a basic red shirt and black pants. They had no problem finding what he wanted, unlike Angel and Mom who would spend hours later looking for the "perfect" outfit. That is why he and Dad went alone and Angel and Mom went at another time together.

After they had finished buying his outfit they had gone to the bookstore. Kyle wanted to get Angel's gift. Remembering how much she writes he got her a professional notebook to hold her stories in and a cool journal he knew she would love. Since he didn't have much money left, afterwards he went to the dollar store to buy her the pen and pencil set to complete the gift. It was a really neat set, professional looking and her favorite color, gold. He couldn't wait to see Angels face when she opened it Christmas morning.

Angel wondered what Kyle was grinning about as she put her homework in her book bag and straightened the desk. It couldn't be about her gift. He always listened to what new book she wanted around Christmas time and got her that. It was predictable, but Angel liked it because she loved to read.

"Kids, dinner's ready. Lasagna tonight, hurry before it gets cold," Mommy called up to Angel and Kyle.

They both looked at each other thinking the same thing. "Yum! Mommy's lasagna was the greatest!"

Walking into the kitchen, Angel saw Daddy sitting at the table reading the classified ads while Mommy put salad in bowls next to plates that already had lasagna and garlic bread on them. It smelled so good. Angel hadn't realized how hungry she really was until she sat down.

"Angel honey, it's your night to get the drinks. Daddy and I will both have a cup of coffee, and pour you and Kyle each a nice glass of milk," Mommy said sitting down.

Angel poured the drinks, carried them to the table and then took her seat. Daddy sat down at the table and the family joined hands. Bowing their heads Daddy recited the prayer.

"Lord, we thank you for this food and all that you have provided. We thank you for Angel being chosen the head angel in the Christmas program and for Kyle receiving a trophy today for football. We thank you for blessing them with wonderful gifts. Thank you for helping us through these difficult times. Bless Grandpa, our family and all our friends. In your name we pray," Daddy said.

"Amen," they all said in unison and dug into the wonderful meal.

Angel and Mommy washed dished while Daddy and Kyle went outside to decorate the front of the house a little more. Daddy had found some more decorations in the basement from a long time ago. It was a mild night, not too cold or windy, so Daddy said he and Kyle would put them up while they went shopping.

Angel finished drying the last dish and put it in the cupboard with a big smile on her face.

"Ok, that's it. You can go up and get ready for bed Angel. I'm going to take a long hot bath and read a book," Mommy said, turning her back to Angel so she couldn't see her grinning.

"Mommy! Nice try you know you can't fool me like that," Angel said laughing and going to get their coats.

Angel and Mommy piled into the car and headed off for the mall that was about 15 miles away. On the way they listened to one of Mommy's country Christmas CDs and sang along with the songs as loud as they could. Laughing and giggling all the way through the words.

After finding a parking spot close to the mall entrance they ran inside. It was getting a little chilly.

"Ok, let's go and see if we can find the perfect dress," Mommy said taking off her gloves.

Angel took her gloves off also, putting them in the pocket of her winter coat.

Looking through racks and racks of dressed in the third shop that night, Angel thought they would never find something they would agree on. Then, she spotted it. In front of her was black velvet dress with a red ribbon for a belt. It was perfect, elegant and beautiful. Angel reached out and took it off the rack.

"Oh, Angel that is beautiful. You will look great in that!" Mommy said.

Angel looked down at the price tag and saw the dress was expensive.

"No, I'll find something else," Angel said.

Mommy took the dress from Angel's grasp and looked at the tag.

"It is a bit much, but I turned in my collection of pop bottles today. It was about $20 so I think this one is doable," Mommy said winking and smiling at Angel.

With a smile Angel took the dress and went into the dressing room while Mommy looked at the nylons. Angel slipped the velvet dress on and looked at her reflection in the mirror. "Mark will love this," she thought to herself. It was perfect!

"Honey, you're so beautiful!" Mommy said when Angel came out to show her the dress and to make sure it fit properly.

Mommy walked around her and pulled down on some areas of the dress. She them smiled, giving the thumbs up. Angel went back into the dressing room, changing into her jeans and sweater. They decided that nude nylons would look best with the dress and Angel would wear Mommy's black low-heeled shoes. With both of them wearing the same shoe size there was not a need to buy new dress shoes. Besides, Mommy had only worn the shoes twice so far and Angel loved them!

"Let's go get a hot chocolate and walk around the mall. We can look at the decorations," Mommy said.

They both got hot chocolate at the food court and began walking around. Angel loved the huge Christmas trees all lit up and glimmering. Then, they came upon Santa's village. Mommy looked at Angel.

"Mommy, I'm too old to sit on Santa's lap! I'll just write him a letter," Angel said.

"Oh, ok. Well, here, hold my drink," Mommy said handing Angel her hot chocolate and purse.

Without a word Mommy went over and sat on Santa's lap. Angel laughed, shaking her head as she walked over to Mommy and Santa.

"Put our stuff down, Angel. I'll get us each a picture with both of us and Santa," Mommy said.

They posed with Santa and Mom bought two pictures.

They finished their drinks and went to the dollar store to get frames. Three dollars later, with two beautiful gold frames holding their pictures, they walked back to the car.

Angel knew this was going to be a small Christmas and was supposed to not be much fun because of their money problems, but so far, she was thinking this was the best Christmas ever. Sitting with Mommy on Santa's lap was fun and the photo in the $1.50 gold frame she held in her hands meant more to her than any gift in the world.

Kyle and Daddy had put tons of lights up outside and there was a Santa's sleigh on the front yard. It looked great! Angel modeled the dress for Daddy and he loved it. She then said she was going up to bed to read. Sitting on her beanbag chair in her flannel pajamas Angel wrote in her journal about the trip to the mall and the talk with Kyle that evening. It had been a great day; and, was looking to be a cool Christmas Season!

CHAPTER FIVE:

Awakening the next morning Angel felt excitement immediately fill her. It was going to be a great day. They had rehearsal for the Christmas play, it was taco day at lunch and her homeroom class was going to plan the class Christmas Party and also draw names for the gift exchange.

What was cool is her teacher was putting all the names in a hat and letting them draw another classmate's name. Each teacher Angel had had before this year sent a note home to the parents telling the girls to bring a girl gift, and boys to bring a boy gift with a $5 limit. That was ok, but Angel missed out on the fun of shopping for one particular person. Looking for the gift you know they would love; and, this year she would be able to do that.

Angel slipped on a pair of jeans and one of her favorite oversized sweaters. It was a rose-colored sweater and Angel put a Christmas pin on too. She seemed to be so filled with the Holiday Spirit this year and didn't know why, but she liked it!

"Hopefully I'll get to choose Jolene, Pam or Christie for the drawing. It will be so easy since I know what they like and know them best out of everyone in the class," Angel thought to herself.

But the girls always gave each other small gift at Christmas. Things that are just a few dollars that they exchange at a little party held at one of their houses. This year would be a small get together at Angel's house as it got closer to Christmas. It was going to be so much fun!

"Angel, time for breakfast," Mommy called up the stairs as

Angel finished putting some small butterfly clips in her hair.

"Coming Mommy," she yelled back.

Angel grabbed her book bag and headed downstairs for breakfast. As she made her way down the stairs the aroma of sausage greeted her. Sitting down at the table Mommy put a plate of biscuits and gravy in front of her with sausage links on the side. Angel poured a glass of milk and waited for Kyle to come down so they could say grace and eat their breakfast. She couldn't wait to get to the bus stop and tell the girls about her time with Mommy at the mall and explain the beautiful dress they had gotten.

"Hi guys!" Angel said once she got to the bus stop.

It was a perfect winter morning, chilly with a dusting of fresh snow covering everything. The girls were freezing and kept their hands in their coat pockets. Angel loved these kinds of mornings; her coat was so warm and her mittens and boots kept her comfortable. The only part of her that always got really cold was her nose.

"We got my dress for the program last night. It is so beautiful guys; it's black with velvet and a red ribbon belt. Mommy is letting me wear her cool low heel shoes that I showed you the other day," Angel said smiling.

"Where did you get the dress?" Christie asked.

"At that new store in the mall. We went there and it just called to me. It was a little more than Mommy wanted to spend but she had some extra cash from somewhere so we got it. Then, we went to look at the decorations and Mommy actually sat on Santa's lap!" Angel said laughing.

All the girls laughed. They knew how fun Mommy was and that it was something they all knew she would do. That is why all Angel's friends liked Mommy so much. She was nice, but also did fun and crazy things sometimes.

"What was cool though is she got each of us a picture with both of us on Santa's lap. Then we went to the dollar store and got these little gold frames. It was so cool and fun," Angel told them.

The bus started pulling up and Angel agreed that she would show them the picture at their Christmas party at her house. Just then Kyle, Randy, Kevin and Denny walked by the girls. Kyle reached over and honked Angel's nose. He always did it when her nose turned red from the cold. Normally she would have yelled at him because she hated it when he did that. But it was actually kind of funny and for some reason they were all laughing and talking as they got on the bus. Usually Kyle and his friends ignored Angel and her friends. But they were talking and laughing, and they all sat near each other that morning.

"Mommy is letting us have our party as a slumber party guys," Angel told the girls as they rode to school.

"Oh, that is so cool. When are we going to have it?" Pam asked.

"Yeah, what day? All we have to decide on now is a day and time," Jolene said, pulling on lipstick again.

"Well, I was thinking we could have it right after the Christmas play. That night you could all just ride home from the play with us," Angel said.

"Cool!" they said in unison.

The bus continued down the street as Angel, Christie Pam, Jolene, Kyle, Randy, Kevin, Keith and Denny talked about Christmas. They were comparing Christmas wish lists as the school came into view.

"Just three more days," Angel thought to herself. It was less than a week before the play, gift exchange and Christmas sleep over. After putting her coat, boots and other winter stuff in her locker, Angel grabbed the books she'd need for the first two classes and headed down the hallway. Stopping at the water fountain she gulped some cold water. She went into the girl's bathroom, brushed her hair and put on a little of Jolene's lipstick and eye shadow. First class was Creative Writing and Mark would be there.

"Good morning all!" Ms. Doyle called to her students as she

walked into the classroom.

Everyone was already in their assigned seats with the assignment from last night on their desks ready to turn in. Ms. Doyle liked to make the most of their time in the classroom and had told everyone the first day of school to have their assignments out and ready to turn in by the time the bell rang.

Angel watched as Ms. Doyle sat down her mug of coffee. She put her bag on the desk and pulled out her attendance book, a notebook where she kept notes and the textbook they used once in a while. Ms. Doyle mainly just had the class journal and write papers; but they did use the books sometimes and got their information to study for tests out of it.

"Ok, attendance time," Ms. Doyle said, taking a drink of coffee and dragging her chair in front of her desk. She sat down, opened the attendance book and put a red pen behind her ear and held onto her black pen.

"Katie," Ms. Doyle called.

"Here," Katie said.

"Jake," Ms. Doyle called.

"Here," Jake said.

This went on for the first few minutes of class. If a student was there Ms. Doyle would put a black check by their name for the day. But if they were gone, they would receive a red check for the day and she would writer their name down on her notebook. She always kept a notebook out for notes or things she remembered during the day.

If you were sick or missed one of Ms. Doyle's classes, she would get all the work you missed and write the assignment down. Then, if you had a sister or brother in the school, she would send it home with them. If you didn't have a sibling in school, she would find a way to get the work to you that night. Sometimes she even took it herself!

As she closed the attendance book Ms. Doyle sighed. She stood up and put the book in her desk. After talking another drink of coffee, she went to the first row of desks.

"Please pass your papers to the front desk. I need your assignments from last night and your journals to be checked," she said.

The room filled with the noise of papers being passed and notebooks being closed and also handed to the student in the front desk of their row. Ms. Doyle walked down the row of desks collecting the papers and notebooks.

"I'll correct these while you work on today's assignment and hand them back at the end of class. Then, we will line up at the door to go to the Christmas Program practice," she said smiling.

She set down the papers and notebooks on her desk and then picked up her notebook. When she turned around there was a big smile. Angel knew this was going to be a great assignment. Whenever Ms. Doyle smiled like that it was always a very creative paper to be written.

"Ok class. I want you to write an essay one what Christmas means to you. Share with me why it is special. What does your family do that means a lot to you? What traditions do you have and what do you think is the real meaning of Christmas? Be creative kids, this is supposed to be a fun assignment," Ms. Doyle said.

"How long does it have to be?" Shane asked.

There were kids who hated writing and always asked how long the assignment had to be. Angel, however, usually had to be careful to not write too much. Sometimes she got carried away and turned in long pieces. Ms. Doyle would sometimes joke with saying the book wasn't due till the end of the year.

"It needs to be a minimum of three pages. And, a maximum of six pages," Ms. Doyle said smiling at Angel.

"I'm going to give you all of class to work on this. So, get started and no talking," she said.

Angel picked up her pen and took out six pieces of loose-leaf paper.

"Christmas can mean so much to different kids. But, to me Christmas is special because of how it feels. I've discovered how strong this feeling is this year because we haven't been able make Christmas about mainly gifts. My Daddy has no job, so money is a problem right now.

"Because of that we have to think hard about gifts we do give. But we have done other fun stuff. Mommy and I took our picture with Santa and got two copies that we put in gold frames. Plus, I have had to think a lot about what my Daddy, Mommy, and Kyle like so I can buy a good gift. I don't know what Christmas will be like, but it will be fun..." Angel wrote.

A half-hour later Angel finished her sixth page of the assignment. Some kids were done, but had only written three pages and made their handwriting very big so it would full up more space. They were whispering a little. Angel pulled out her horse folder and put the assignment in it. She would go over it tonight at home to see if she needed to change anything. Then, she would rewrite it to hand in tomorrow.

"The bell is going to ring soon. As I call your name please pick up your journal and take it and your books to your lockers. Then come right back here. No going to the drinking fountain or restroom. Get your coats and boots and come back to the classroom. We will walk over to the church for rehearsal as soon as the bell rings," Ms. Doyle said.

One by one each of the students' names were called out. Angel could hear the slamming of locker doors and laughter. Each of the boys and girls in her class came back in with their winter wear on and took their spot in line. Finally, Angel's name was called and she hurried to her locker.

When she came back into the classroom Ms. Doyle had finished calling names and was slipping on her long coat. Angel took her place in line. In front of her were Pam and Jolene and behind her was Christie. They always ended up in line together like this.

Angel watched Ms. Doyle take out her gloves and slip them on. After looking up at the clock she realized it was about time for the bell to ring. All the students took the clue from their teacher and put on their gloves. Finally, the bell sounded and Ms. Doyle led them out the side doors of the school.

Everyone followed her down the sidewalk to the stop sign. They all waited for the students in the back of the line to get to the stop sign. Ms. Doyle then walked out to the middle of the road to make sure traffic was stopped and the students crossed the street to St. John Church. As they got to the building Angel looked back and saw Kyle's class just getting to the stop sign.

Each class took their appointed place in the pews. They all had specific spots they sat in when there were all-school masses. With everyone in the school being there for rehearsal it was easiest to have them sit in those places.

First, the little Kindergarten kids put on the signs they had made. In art class they had made signs which now hung from their necks by yarn. Each sign had a pretty drawing that the student had colored. Some were of Christmas trees and gifts while others were of nativity scenes and angels. The class sang "Joy to the World" and "Jingle Bells".

Then, the first through fifth grade joined them. They sang several songs including "We Three Kings" and "All I Want for Christmas is My Two Front Teeth". Each year the classes sang basically the same songs. They were songs Angel had sung for the past six years. All the sixth graders sang along with them. Then it was their turn.

The Kindergarten through Fifth Grade students walked off the altar and back to their pews. Fr. Joe recited the story of the first Christmas from the Bible. The Sixth-Grade students then went to the front. Ms. Doyle handed out their costumes. Angel slipped on her flowing robe made from a white sheet. There was garland attached along the bottom of the sheet and around the end of the sleeves. She also had a headpiece made of garland that was her halo. Everyone took their places. Fr. Joe then talked more about the true meaning of the holiday and introduced the Sixth-Grade nativity scene.

All the students walked onto the altar. The angels' choir stood very still in the adult choir area. Jackie and Mark took their place in the wooden replica of the stable with Jackie holding the baby once again. Angel stood behind them. The whole class sang "Mary had a Baby" and "O' Little Town of Bethlehem". Pam then sang "The First Noel". As an ending to the play the Kindergarten through Fifth Grade sat in front of the altar and joined in on a few more songs. The last song everyone sang was "Silent Night".

The whole practice took near an hour and a half. Everyone put on their coats and headed back to the school. After putting her coat in her locker, Angel got her science book and walked to the science room. This class lasted until lunch. The day had gone by so fast!

It seemed to Angel that Science drug on forever. They were learning about plants. It didn't interest Angel like art and writing did. Science was her most difficult course, but she worked hard and was getting a B. Finally, the bell rang and Pam, Christie, Jolene, and Angel started walking to the lunchroom.

The aroma of tacos greeted the girls. They all loved tacos. It was the best meal, after pizza of course. Angel took two milks, her silverware and napkin and then handed her ticket to the lunch lady. Mrs. Bundy punched her ticket and Angel took a tray. She chose a couple tacos and pears. For desert was chocolate cake. Angel was the first one through the line, so she went to their normal table and took her spot. The girls all took a seat one by one and they started planning their party.

"We've only got three days so we better decide what we want to eat and what movies to get," Pam said.

"Well, Mommy made a bunch of treats when she made our Christmas goodies so we have those. I was thinking about getting some chocolate milk for hot chocolate and marshmallows. We can also have eggnog and for supper hamburgers and French fries," Angel said.

"That sounds great! But, what movies should we get?" Christie said taking a bite out of her taco.

"They have to be Christmas flicks. How about 'Look Who's Talking Now' and 'Christmas in Connecticut'?" Jolene asked.

"Yeah I love those movies!" Angel said.

During lunch the girls decided on a list of movies to reserve. They would pick them up on the way home from the play. Pam, Christie and Jolene also decided to bring their overnight things to the play and would put them in the SUV before or right after.

"This is going to be so much fun!" Angel said.

But a sinking feeling came to Angel. It would be no problem getting the girls gifts because she had been saving her money from babysitting Uncle Mike's baby. But, they would for sure notice that there were not many gifts under the family tree. They had come over before when Daddy had been working and had seen tons of gifts. How would she explain it?

"God, please help. Please make this a great Christmas and don't make the girls feel sorry for me when they see how many fewer gifts we have under the tree," Angel prayed.

The bell sounded, letting the students know that it was time to put their trays back and get to their next class. Angel finished her milk and threw away her garbage. She put the tray up on the container and heard someone say "hi" behind her. Turning, she saw Mark standing there.

"Hi," she said.

"So, what did you think about Ms. Doyle's Creative Writing assignment?" Mark asked.

"I like it. I've got six pages done and am going to go over it tonight. Probably will rewrite it before I hand it in tomorrow morning," Angel said.

"You are a great writer, Angel. I love writing too, just wish I could be as good as you are," Mark said.

"I'm not that good at it. It's just something I like and seems to come naturally for me. It's one subject that doesn't seem hard. I have to work as hard as I can, to get okay grades in my other classes," Angel told him.

"Well, I like the way your write. Your stories are my favorite in our class," Mark said.

Mark and Angel walked together to the sixth-grade lockers. Angel's was first. She stopped to grab her books and Mark waited. Then, they stopped at Mark's locker before making their way down the hall to their next class, Iowa History.

When they walked in together laughing and talking Angel could see the girls watching them. Mark told her he had better go say hi to his friends before class started and went to the other side of the room to his assigned seat. Angel went to her seat that was right next to Christie, Pam, and Jolene.

CHAPTER SIX:

"Ok, tell us everything!" Jolene said smiling as the other girls leaned closer to hear the whole story.

"It's nothing. He just asked me about the assignment in Creative Writing. He told me he liked my stories the best and was wondering if I'd gotten the assignment done," Angel said as she took out her notebook, pen and opened her text book to the chapter they had been assigned to read the night before.

"Good afternoon class. Please open your books the last nights chapter and take out you notebook and pens. We're going to discuss the main ideas highlighted in the chapter," Mr. Hocking said.

He sat down his briefcase and opened the Social Studies book on his desk. After taking off his sports coat he took a piece chalk and wrote down Chapter 12 on the board. He then wrote the five main points and started his lecture over Iowa History.

After what seemed like hours, but was only a half-hour of Iowa History, Angel took her books back to her locker. Next was Math with Ms. Doyle and the class would be drawing names and planning their Christmas party.

"Hope lunch was ok. How was Iowa History?" Ms. Doyle asked.

Sitting down at her desk she took the cap off her black pen, put the red one behind her ear and opened her attendance book again. She read off the students' names, down the list one by one. She put a black or red mark by each name, depending on whether they were present or absent.

"Well, now with that being done, everyone take out a sheet of loose leaf paper and pencil. We're going to have a quiz over what we've been studying this week. I hope you all did your homework last night," Ms. Doyle said.

Ms. Doyle then wrote down 10 problems on the chalk-board and stepped back, making sure she had correctly written down the numbers. Nodding to herself she told the class to begin.

Angel was very good at writing, art and language classes. She had also started taking a literature class that she loves; but Math was just one of those subjects which was difficult for her. She struggled in Science, but Math was worse.

"Please, Lord, be with me during this quiz. I've studied this stuff so many times, but I'm not sure I've got it. Mommy helped me last night with these kinds of problems and I was doing ok when we finished. Please help me be calm and think these through," Angel prayed before starting to work the first problem.

Ever since first grade Angel prayed before each test or quiz. She was always so nervous when tests were given, especially pop quizzes. Praying seemed to help a lot and she knew the Lord was there helping her out. He was always there and always would be. She knew this in her heart.

A few minutes the quizzes were traded and the class corrected their neighbor's papers while Ms. Doyle worked the problems on the board. Angel traded with Christie and was not surprised that Christie had gotten each problem right. She was so good at Math. Angel traded papers back with Christie and let out a sigh of relief when she saw she had only missed one problem. Whew!

"Ok, now it's time to draw names and plan our Christmas party," said Ms. Doyle

She went on to explain that she had a red stocking that she had put a slip with each student's name in. Each student would draw a name from the stocking and would have to write the name down on a piece of paper. Then, they would go around the room saying what they like to do and the types of gifts they would like.

It wasn't a wish list, just helping the person who drew their name know more about them and what they like. It would make shopping easier. They would also not tell each other who they drew. It was going to be a "Secret Santa" and they would need to leave little notes or little tokens of happiness in their person's desk or locker. Ms. Doyle asked them to creative, to make it really fun. Leaving candy was ok, but it was not to be eaten during class.

It took a few minutes, but finally Ms. Doyle and her stocking made their way to Angel. She reached into the red stocking and pulled out a slip. Opening it up she could not believe what she saw written on the paper.

Mark Adams

She had drawn Mark's name. Never did she think she might draw a boy's name, let along Mark Adams. But it was a nice surprise. When they got to Mark and he said he liked writing, books and rodeo. Angel began thinking what she could get for him. She knew tomorrow her first "Secret Santa" message would be a rodeo poem her Mommy had written and she would wrap one of Daddy's old horseshoes and put it on Mark's desk before class. He'd love it. The rodeo poem would be perfect, because he loved reading and rodeo, and the horseshoe would bring good luck.

"Ok, everyone. Write down what your person said and put your paper in your take home folders. Now, let's plan the party!" Ms. Doyle said.

After a half-hour of planning the class had decided that they would play Christmas music during the party and have a bunch of Christmas goodies and punch. Jackie had offered to bring a jug of her Daddy's special Christmas punch made of fruit punch, orange juice and 7-Up mixed together. They also decided that they would put up some decorations during recess for the party. Angel was bringing everyone's favorite, her Mommy's

Christmas goodies. Pam was bringing her Mom's homemade sugar cookies; Jolene was in charge of Christmas CDs and Mark was going to bring plates and napkins. Each student had a job or item to bring by the end of the meeting.

The bell signaling that school was over finally rang. Angel thought to herself that she only had two days to go shopping and find gifts not only for her friends, but now for Mark too!

When she came through the door Angel saw Mommy was waiting outside. That meant one thing, shopping. The Lord had once again known what Angel needed and made sure Mommy was waiting for her. He was always looking out for everyone and helping everyone whom needed it.

"Guess I'm not talking the bus home girls," Angel told her friends.

"Oh, I see. There's your mother. Shopping time!" Pam said giggling.

"I want jewelry, a CD player, and one thousand dollars," Jolene said laughing too.

"Catch ya tomorrow, Angel. Give me a call tonight so we can talk more about the party if you want," Christie said.

Jolene and Pam both told Angel to call them too. But, of course, there was not a night where she didn't call each of her friends. They were her life and each time she talked to them, she was happy.

"So, you ready to go Christmas shopping? You know I'm one of those people who do last minute shopping. We have a lot to do," Mommy said.

"Cool, I've got some to do. But, shoot! I don't have my money on me. At home I have fifty bucks stashed away from babysitting," Angel said.

"That's ok, Angel. I'll just take fifty out at the ATM, and you can give me your fifty when we get home. This way we won't have to go back there. We can go straight to the mall instead. And, Daddy and Kyle are going to a father and son thing tonight. So, how bout we get a bite to eat at a buffet place? How about Chinese?" Mommy said.

"Okay! I 've got to get a gift for Kyle, Christie, Pam, and Jolene. And, today I drew Mark Adam's name for Secret Santa. He said he likes rodeo, writing and reading. So, I thought I'd get him a writing tablet, some folders with horses or rodeo stuff on the covers and a nice pen and pencil set. Then, I'd wrap up each of them separate and tie them together with a nice ribbon.

"We're supposed to leave little notes or gifts until Friday when we have our class party. I think I'm going to leave him a note with one of your rodeo poems on it if that's ok. I'm also going to wrap up one of Daddy's old horseshoes he doesn't use anymore and leave it on his desk. What do you think?" Angel said.

Angel buckled her seat belt after getting in the SUV. Mommy was already buckled up and putting a Christmas CD in the stereo. Christmas carols filled the vehicle as they set off for the mall.

"I think that is great, Angel. Do you know what you want to get your brother?" Mommy asked.

"Yep, I'm going to get Kyle a book I saw at the bookstore about football. And, there is also a little calendar thing with football teams I think he'd like," Angel said.

"So, do you know Mark very well? I know his name for some reason," Mommy said signaling to enter the interstate.

"Well, he's the guy who's playing Joseph in the play," Angel said blushing.

"No, I know why. He's the one you think is cute and you like. He talked to you the other day, and you told me all about it," Mommy said.

"Okay, yes that too," Angel said giggling.

They continued driving to the mall singing Christmas carols. It was cold outside, but nice and warm in the SUV and Angel was having so much fun. When Mommy took the CD out a weather report was on the radio. The forecast was for two to four inches of snow overnight. Maybe they'd have a late start tomorrow. That way Angel could sleep in and classes wouldn't be as long; but more than likely there wouldn't be, and she would have to get up early for school.

Mommy and Angel spent the next few hours going store to store buying gifts. They got one for Daddy, one for Grandpa, and one for Kyle. Angel also purchased her friend's gifts. She couldn't wait for the slumber party that was so close. But first would be the class Christmas Party. Then there would be the program with the slumber party following.

It was all going by so fast, but this year Angel had noticed that Christmas was different, like it had a new meaning. She was having fun shopping for everyone and planning the different events. This year she wasn't paying so much attention on what she wanted. Angel was having so much fun giving gifts to others. As each day passed Angel was learning the true meaning of Christmas!

Friday arrived faster than Angel had expected. She awoke that morning to a fresh snowfall. It was a perfect day for a Christmas party. The night before she and Mommy had baked tons of goodies and she had wrapped Mark's present. She knew he was going to love it.

When he had seen the rodeo poem and lucky horseshoe, he had been so excited. It was amazing how good giving someone something they wanted felt. This year Angel had been more in tune to the real meaning of the holiday. The Christmas spirit had filled her for the first time in her life.

"Angel time to get up, rise and shine. The bus will be here soon!" Mommy called up the stairs like she did every morning.

"Coming Mommy, just let me finish getting dressed," Angel said.

Because Angel loved Christmas so much, she had tons of holiday clothes. She chose a black pair of jeans, a red sweater with snowmen on it and a white turtleneck underneath. She finished off her outfit with her favorite black cowgirl boots. It was going to be a great day!

After finishing a delicious breakfast, Angel rushed to the bus stop. During the bus ride she and her friends talked about the day which awaited them.

"I just can't wait to see who drew my name. I'm totally stumped," Christie said.

"Me too, everyone was so sneaky this year!" Pam laughed.

Angel looked over and saw that Jolene was in the middle of the novel she'd been reading. She only had started it a few days before and was almost done with it. Romance novels were her favorite, and more than likely, Jolene would get some for Christmas.

The bus stopped in front of St. John and all the kids grabbed their book bags and gifts. All the students in Angel's class hurried to their lockers. Coats and winter wear were quickly hung as everyone headed for the classroom. Angel's mouth dropped open as she took her seat.

Their classroom had been transformed into a winter wonderland. Decorations were everywhere. Greenery, tinsel, ornaments, lights and stocking hung from desks, tables, shelves and even the ceiling. The pencil sharpener was even decorated with wrapping paper and ribbon! The best part was the tree.

"I hope you all like the decorations. Last night, I was in the holiday mood, and thought this would be great for our class party. I hope you all remembered your gifts today. To start the morning, I will call your names. While I mark you down as here today, each of you can place your gift under the tree. Then, I will hand back your papers from Creative Writing yesterday. Today, I want you all to write a short story about Christmas," Ms. Doyle said as she took out her attendance book.

A few minutes later there were gifts under the tree and everyone was in a great mood. Now they were all working on their papers. Then, it was off to Math and Science. After lunch the party would begin. The day would then finish up with Music and Art. Angel could hardly wait for the party. She just knew Mark would love the gifts she had bought him, and she was very curious about who had drawn her name. Over the past week she had received a lot of nice notes and candy each day.

A few hours later the class was working on their Science projects and lab work when the lunch bell rang. The morning had gone by fast. Angel grabbed a burger, fries and milk shake, then headed to the table they always sat at. She said her noon prayer thanking the Lord for not only the food, but also the great day. She then said another prayer, wishing Christmas would be great this year. Lastly, she thanked him for making so much wonderful things happen already during this year's holiday season.

All the girls ate quickly and dumped their trays. Then, they headed outside to the playground. The sixth-grade class was allowed fifteen minutes each day after lunch outside. It was nice to get fresh air and take a break. Excitement was in the air as all the students stood around talking about the party.

Finally, the bell rang and everyone headed in. All the kids took their seats and using the attendance book, their names were called once again. When their name was called, they were to go get the gifts they had bought for the person they drew and give it to them at their desk. This way the whole class would know who had drawn whom.

Angel sat at her desk with excitement and anticipation causing nervous knots in her stomach. She couldn't wait to get her gift so she could see who had her. Most of all she couldn't wait to give her gift to Mark.

Over the past few weeks, she went from sadness because it was going to be a small Christmas with a few gifts to being filled with the Holiday Spirit and much happiness. This was the best Christmas she had ever had. Buying gifts was even more fun than opening them. The true spirit of the holiday, giving to others, had filled her completely. She knew it would be a great Christmas. She had faith in God and knew He'd be there for her and her family and everyone who needed him. In her heart she knew God loved everyone completely and would provide anything they truly needed.

"Angel Johnson," Ms. Doyle called out.

This was it; Angel went to the tree and picked up her beautiful wrapped package. She had wrapped and open box and attached curled ribbon to the sides. Then, she's wrapped each gift; the rodeo folders, the pen set and a cool notebook she had found. And, she'd made a folder of Mommy's rodeo poems into a book. She'd typed them all and made a cover. It looked great; she hoped Mark would like it.

Angel walked across the room as the whole class watched. She went to Mark's desk and handed him the box.

"Merry Christmas, Mark," Angel said smiling.

"Thanks! Merry Christmas to you too, Angel," Mark replied.

Angel noticed he had a different type of smile. Not a "thanks for the gift" smile, but an "I know something you don't" smile. Angel wondered what was up as she watched the kids hand out gifts. They would be opening them all at the same time. For now, they were just handing out each gift.

"Mark Adams," the teacher called.

Mark went over to the tree and took out a very beautiful box. He crossed the room as Angel watched. Then, there he was, stopping in front of her desk and handing her the gift in his hands.

"Merry Christmas, Angel! It's neat, we drew each other's names," he said.

The rest of the gifts were handed out and the class began tearing open the wrapping paper to get to the contents of the package before them Angel carefully opened hers so she could save the paper. She looked across the room. Mark was tearing into his faster than anyone else did in the room. Angel giggled as she continued to open hers.

Finally, Angel got to the contents. Her box contained a book about angels and a pretty journal and pen. She loved it! Opening the book she found Mark had written something inside.

Angel,

You were named perfect because you are nice and sweet, just like angels are supposed to be. I'm happy you were lead angel with me in the Christmas program and am glad we are friends. Merry Christmas!

Mark

Angel watched her friends open their gifts. Christie received a book about horses she was very excited about. Jolene was given lip-gloss and body glitter she adored. And, Pam also got a journal and pen/pencil set. Everyone in class was pleased with their gifts.

"Class, pick up your wrapping paper and throw it away; then, take out what you have brought for the party, and we'll have some refreshments and music. You can all visit and talk until it's time for rehearsal. Be sure to thank the person who had your name for you gift," the teacher said.

Everyone began cleaning up their desks and chatting about the gifts they'd been given. Angel and Pam went down to the teacher's lounge to get the goodies. When they got back everything was set up. There were festive napkins, plates, cups and silverware on the table. Chex mix and some other goodies were already set out. Christmas music was playing on the CD player and everyone was singing along. Angel loved class Christmas parties.

"Angel, thanks for the gift," Mark said.

It was a great and fun party, one of the best the class had ever had.

CHAPTER SEVEN:

It was the day of the Christmas play and the family was busy getting ready. Not only did they need to get their clothes and costumes together, but Angel also had to get ready for the slumber party which followed the play. Christmas was so close. As each day passed, Angel and Kyle filled with a little more excitement and anticipation. This was a truly magical season, and this year the Johnson family felt very blessed, even though there was not much money for material things. They were blessed because they had a happy wonderful family, food for Christmas dinner and a lot of love.

"Mommy where is the wrapping stuff?" Angel called down the stairs. She was holding her friends' gifts.

"In my bedroom on the card table, everything you need will the there. You can use our room to wrap gifts if you want," Mommy called back to Angel.

Christmas was approaching at a fast speed. Mommy spent most of her free time with holiday preparations. She not only had to get the house cleaned and ready for the slumber party the following night, but Grandpa would be arriving that night to spend the holidays.

Angel wrapped all the girl's gifts and Kyle's. Kyle's gift was easy, a book on football and a jersey of his favorite team. For Christie there was a journal and a nice pen along with a boot from her favorite author on horses. Pam was getting a book of songs and a couple CDs from her favorite artist. For Jolene Angel had gotten a great make up case filled with make up. It was so fun picking out the colors and shades.

"Now, what kind of paper; do I do them in different typed or all the same?" Angel asked herself. She finally decided on one; a very sophisticated shiny red paper with huge white ribbons. After near an hour all were wrapped and looked great. Angel had even made her own labels for the packages. She placed them in a gift bag to carry to the tree. She set Kyle's next to Grandpa's but left the girls in the gift bag. She would give them their gifts during the slumber party that night.

There were great smells coming from the kitchen Angel poked in to see Mommy cooking up a storm. It smelled like her special beef stew. Grandpa loved it. Mommy always made Grandpa some to take home with him and freeze.

"You want a snack?" Mommy called when she noticed Angel standing in the doorway. "I have tons here!" she said laughing.

"Nah, think I'll do some journaling and then take a bubble back before the play," Angel said.

"What book is it this time?" Mommy asked. Angel always soaked in a bubble bath with a book.

"A Christmas Story," Angel said laughing.

Angel went to her room and wrote about her day in her journal. All about wrapping gifts, why she chose those special gifts and how she hoped everyone would love them. When she had finished, she had filled nearly four pages.

Angel began getting ready for the Christmas Program. She put on the beautiful dress Mommy had bought and walked down the stairs carefully since she was wearing small heels for the first time in her life. It made her feel so much older. Grandpa was standing there and bowed as she walked down the stairway, whistling and holding out his arm for her to take. Grandpa always did stuff like that. Angel put on her dress coat as Kyle walked down in his new suit and tie. The whole family looked so dressed up. Angel thought to herself that this was one of the best parts of the program.

Daddy, Mommy, Grandpa Angel and Kyle piled into the family SUV and heading for St John Church where the program would be held. Candles lit the church to the point it was almost glowing. Angel and Kyle said goodbye to their parents in the entryway of the church and went to the basement to meet their classes.

The girls were all there and dressed up. Mark looked so great in his suit and tie. Angel's knees were buckling and her legs felt like jelly. She had never had a crush this big on a boy.

"Hey Angel, you look beautiful tonight," Mark said as she turned around.

"Thanks Mark, you look handsome," she said.

The baby started fussing with Jackie so Angel and Mark walked over. Angel took the baby and quieted him. She was the only one who could keep him quiet and calm.

"I love Christmas," Angel said.

"Thanks for the presents. They were great. I love your Mom's poetry. Does she have a book or been in magazines?" he asked.

"She used to write for magazines and had a couple books published; but, now has decided to raise my brother and me until she can trust us on our own. You know, because of book signings or book tours," Angel said with a smile.

"That is so cool," Mark said.

Finally, all the classes lined up and the sixth-grade students put on their costumes. The play was about to begin.

The program was wonderful. The baby barely fussed and all the songs were beautiful. After an hour the whole congregation joined in singing "Silent Night" while everyone held a lit candle. The church was aglow.

And, Santa came at the end. All the younger elementary students lined up to tell Santa what they wanted him to bring on

Christmas Eve and receives a candy cane.

Christie, Jolene, and Pam had their things waiting in the parents' cars, so after the program everyone loaded into the SUV and the slumber party officially started. The girls were giggly and loud all the way home. Once inside they saw that Mommy had done her magic again.

There were plates of fudge, peanut clusters, cookies and any Christmas goody you could imagine. The table was decorated like a Christmas gift and Mommy had put a thermos of hot chocolate on the table with everything else. The girls all loaded up their plates and poured big cups of hot chocolate with marshmallow cream.

There was always a tradition to these parties. Hog out on the yummiest food while watching movies. There were five of their favorites; "Miracle on 34th Street", "The Grinch that Stole Christmas", "All I Want for Christmas", "Home for the Holidays" and "Jingle All the Way" on top of the DVD player when they walked into the family room.

The sleeping bags were rolled out and popcorn was being popped over the fire in the fireplace. Mommy and Daddy had made it perfect. They always did. There were three people Angel could always rely on; Mommy, Daddy, and the Lord.

The girls quickly settled in and started munching and going through the thermos of hot chocolate by the second movie. Then they switched to the soda pop which had been specially purchased for the slumber party. Between the third and fourth movie the girls decided to exchange gifts.

Mommy, Daddy, Kyle, and his friends all came to the tree. Mommy and Daddy had gotten Pam, Jolene, and Christie gifts too as well as Kyle's friends, Keith, Denny, Randy, and Kevin. The gifts were handed out with each person having two to open.

Next, a hat was passed around and the person who drew the paper with a picture of Jesus on it was chosen to open their gift. First was Jolene, she loved the makeup kit and started looking at the colors right away. Next, Mommy drew and when she opened her gift, she found a new nativity scene. It made her cry, she loved it so much. Next, Kyle opened a football book. Then, the rest opened their gifts. What Pam gave Angel touched her so much. It was the most precious snow globe with an angel whose wings were spread. It also played the song "Angels Among Us". It was the best gift of the night.

Throughout the next three movies the boys kept running in and out of the family room teasing the girls. But when the fire started to go out in the fireplace, it was Kyle who fixed it so they'd stay warm. Kyle didn't know Angel was still awake, but when he thought she was asleep, he pulled the cover up so she would stay warm. He was very protective.

The girls woke the next morning to the smell of pancakes, sausage, bacon, eggs and Texas Toast. Wow! It smelled so very good. The girls jumped up, put on their robes and slippers and ran to the kitchen. Mommy and Daddy had cooked a feast. Kyle and his friends were there too.

Everyone ate and talked about the excitement of the day. It was *Christmas Eve*. The Johnson's' didn't put much emphasis on Santa. Christmas was a holiday to celebrate the birth of Jesus Christ. Instead of reading only the <u>Night before Christmas,</u> the family also read the story of the first Christmas from the bible. Before breakfast a prayer was said and they all wished Jesus an early Happy Birthday. The nativity scene Mommy was given was set up in the kitchen. It was a great start to a special day.

After the girls went home carrying not only the gift's they'd been given, but also a tray of goodies for their families, the Johnson family got into gear. There was so much to be done. First, they prepared the foods that could be done in advance. It helped Mommy out a lot with dinner on Christmas day. The main part of Christmas Eve for Mommy was spent in the kitchen and out shopping for last minute items.

Dad kicked back and made his list. He always looked forward to looking at lights each night and making sure the house twinkled. It hurt Daddy knowing that this wouldn't be a Christmas like the ones he had given in the past, but he had faith in the Lord to help him out. He put the problems at the foot of the Lord knowing that Christmas would happen.

The mailman arrived shortly midmorning. Daddy went to get the bazillion Christmas Cards that were waiting for the family. One was from his old college friend. He usually sent a package. This puzzled Daddy so he opened it immediately. The card explained his friend had been ill. He was fine now; however, was unable to do any shopping. So, he sent $50 instead.

Daddy's eyes lightened. He would not tell anyone in the family. This would be the Christmas surprise; the prayer he'd been waiting to have answered. So, off he went shopping. They knew that Grandpa had helped them have a Christmas but this would help even more. Reading through the paper he went to the auction being held that day.

Cars were everywhere. Daddy parked a mile away and walked to the building. He purchased a cup of coffee and grabbed his bidding paddle. After hours of what looked to be junk, a box was brought up to the auctioneer. There was a box of wonderful china. It would be prefect for Mommy. He bid five-dollars and someone went to six. He thought it would go high, but Daddy won the box for only ten-dollars.

He was so happy; the Lord was looking out for him. He also bid on a football jersey for Kyle that he won. A group of antique books for Angel, and he won a box of tools for Grandpa. With the little money he had left, he purchased some last-minute gifts at the dollar store as well as picking up extra wrapping paper. This would be a Christmas the family would never forget.

The garage was his secret shop as he brought in the bags from the dollar store and also the boxes from the auction. He locked the door and got to work.

CHAPTER EIGHT:

Daddy quickly cleaned off an old workbench. He put the wrapping paper, ribbons, and tags on it. Then, he put the first box containing Mommy's beautiful china, on the table. He took a piece carefully out of the battered box, wrapping it in newspaper. Next, he set the pieces in a Christmas box. When he was finished with all the china and had the box almost taped together, he felt so happy.

So many prayers had been sent up to the Maker. Daddy had wanted so bad to be able to give his family a wonderful Christmas. Things weren't looking very good and with it being so near to Christmas Eve he had been praying harder than ever. He'd given the problem to the Lord, left it in his hands, and it had worked. The Lord had worked his magic once again, providing their family with a Christmas. First, when they were given the money by Grandpa and then with the auction. This was why Daddy never questioned his faith, for he knew the Lord was there and would help.

Daddy picked up the old tattered box to throw it away before anyone found it, when he suddenly noticed it wasn't empty. He looked down and found three of the most beautiful dolls in the bottom of the box. They looked old, but with some cleaning up they would be perfect for Angel. Daddy cleaned them off and hid them in the old car which no longer ran. No one would find them there.

Next was Kyle's gift. Daddy wrapped it in a huge box and threw in his old football gear for him. He'd been asking for it for a long time. Mommy's was beautifully wrapped and Grandpa's was done wonderfully.

Daddy hid the rest by Angel's dolls. That was a problem; there was no way to wrap the dolls. He'd just have to set them out for her. Christmas was looking up after all.

Daddy walked back in the house to the smell of Mommy baking. Every year she spent all day Christmas Eve cooking so she wouldn't have to do everything on Christmas morning. She was still baking cookies, candies and cakes. Actually, it was more like replacing what the family had eaten. It would take a couple hours. Then she'd do potatoes; prepare the turkey to be put in the over in the morning and whatever else she could do ahead of time. Angel and Kyle were watching "Miracle on 34th Street" with Grandpa. Daddy quietly slipped upstairs to finish his wrapping.

"Dinner," Mommy called as she put a hot pot of her special homemade chili on the table.

"Cool, chili," Kyle said as he took his seat at the table.

As the family gathered around the table for their annual Christmas Eve Chili Dinner the phone rang.

"Daddy, it's for you," Angel called.

Everyone sat waiting for Daddy to finish with his phone call. They all were wondering who would be calling on Christmas Eve.

Daddy finally returned to the dining room, wearing a huge smile.

"That was my friend, George. We went to high school to-gether, and he knew I was looking for work," Daddy explained. "He needs a manager for his store in town and needs the person to start immediately. I got a job!" Daddy yelled.

Mommy jumped up holding and kissing him, while the rest of the family hugged him. The Lord works and when left to him he will solve the problem in time.

Dinner had gone very fast, everyone ate Mommy's special chili and had seconds. Angel ran to get the bible while Mommy was clearing the table. After putting the dishes in the dishwasher, she made cups of hot chocolate for them all. Then, the family went to the living room to hear Daddy read from the bible.

Daddy began and not one spoke. He told of the manger, Mary and Joseph. From the bible, he read of the three kings and how there was no room at the inn. He finished with how baby Jesus had been born that night and is now in heaven with His father, the King of Kings, the Lord of Lords.

Next, Daddy read "The Night before Christmas". Angel preferred the story of the first Christmas and Jesus' birth; but she liked this story too.

Time passed quickly. Daddy and Mommy gave both Angel and Kyle a gift to open; new pajamas. Angel loved flannel nightgowns and this one was very soft. She quickly put it on and slipped into bed so she'd be asleep when Santa came to leave his gifts. Kyle and Angel made one last check to see their stockings were up and that milk and cookies were out for Santa. Then, they drifted off to sleep thinking of Christmas morning.

Angel knew it was not going to be like Christmas the years before. There wouldn't be a lot of gifts, but the Christmas spirit was definitely alive in the house. They were all feeling the real meaning of the season; and, she had faith. Faith that the Lord would help them have a few gifts. And soon Santa would arrive, bringing with a gift and special goodies too.

Christmas dawned with a new layer of snow. Angel rolled over and saw one of her gifts sitting on her chair next to her. Three of the most beautiful dolls were sitting there with a note from Daddy and Mommy. They were so pretty.

Angel sat up and looked at each doll more carefully. One even played music. It had a green dress of silk. One was bigger than the other two and had a white dress with blue flowers. She wore a hat and had a hoop skirt that flowed out. The other was the smallest of all but had a face that was hand painted. It wore a crocheted dress and was called a rubber band doll. They were perfect and made Angel's Christmas even before she got out of bed!

Grandpa had lit a fire in the fireplace and Mommy had hot fresh cinnamon rolls waiting along with hot chocolate, coffee and orange juice. The smell of turkey roasting drifted through the house. It was definitely Christmas!

Angel glanced into the living room from the dining room where they were eating. There were so many gifts! Lots more than she expected; but it didn't matter as much. She was just happy to be celebrating Christmas with her parents, brother, and grandfather. The true spirit of Christmas had been found in her heart.

After breakfast the family made their way into the living room where the tree they had cut down and decorated together stood. Beneath were brightly wrapped packages. Angel was chosen to hand out gifts. First, Angel and Kyle unwrapped what Santa had left them. The latest in a series of books Angel had been reading was left for her, while Kyle was given a wood burning kit, which he also loved to do.

Next Angel handed Grandpa his gifts. Instead of doing one gift at a time all the gifts were handed out to the person and everyone would watch them open each one.

Grandpa was happy to get the tools from Daddy and Mommy. He loved the books from Angel and Kyle. The chest from Daddy and Mommy that had a horse blanket in it was very special. It had made him cry; it was just like the one they had had when Daddy was growing up.

Next was mommy's turn. Kyle and Angel had given her new leather gloves, a nice hat and a scarf to match. She loved them! When she opened Daddy's gift, she had tears in her eyes. He gave her the same kind of perfume she wore when they had first been married. The perfume was inside a jewelry box he had made himself.

Grandpa gave her a makeup set and lace. Mommy loved

the lace and hugged Grandpa for remembering a moment in her childhood that involved the same type of lace. When she opened Daddy's other gift her mouth dropped open. Inside a beautiful Christmas box was the china set Daddy had found.

"Well, we now know what we'll be serving Christmas dinner on," she said with a laugh. Mommy had never owned china and now felt so happy.

Daddy also loved his hat, scarf and gloves from Kyle and Angel. Grandpa gave him a very special pocket watch that had belonged to Grandpa's father. Mommy gave Daddy a picture of them at their engagement party that was framed; and, as a surprise to him everyone gave him more wood and supplies for his woodworking.

Kyle loved his football book and calendar. And, he was so happy to have Daddy's old hear with a new jersey. Grandpa gave him a set of books about football; so, basically almost everything Kyle received Christmas morning had something to do with football, which was good. It was his most favorite thing in the world. He also got a pocketknife along with some other little gifts in his stocking.

Angel was thrilled with her dolls but took her turn last to open the gifts under the tree for her. First, she went up and brought down the dolls to show everyone. Her first gift was from Daddy and Mommy, the set of antique books. She loved them and ran her hands over the front covers. Old books were so cool! Kyle gave her the journal and pen/pencil set. The journal was fuzzy and really neat. Grandpa gave her a portfolio to put her finished stories in and some recent copies of writer's magazines. She also got a necklace and a few trinkets in her stocking from Santa.

After everyone was finished opening their gifts Angel and Kyle put the wrappings in a box to be recycled. When they were done it was time for dinner. Mommy had cooked so much. The Lord had helped them by making sure they had a fine meal and a few gifts on Christmas morning. As Angel looked at the beautiful lit tree and Mommy's nativity scene sitting there, she knew that even if there were no gifts, she would have felt the same way.

You see, Christmas isn't gifts and decorations. It is what is in your heart. It's the Christmas spirit when you embrace it. Though not easy to explain, when it does happen to you, you'll know. It's baking a birthday cake and singing Happy Birthday to Jesus. It's singing
"Silent Night" at the school Christmas program with the only light being from candles everyone is holding. It's that peacefully, happy warm feeling.

Angel never gave up. Her faith in the Lord kept her going. She found Jesus along the way and knows fully He loves her unconditionally. Angel thought to herself there was only one more thing to do.

She stood up, raised her glass of milk, and said "Happy Birthday Jesus!"

Printed in Great Britain
by Amazon